SHOW AND TELL BUNNIES

BY KATHRYN LASKY

ILLUSTRATED BY MARYLIN HAFNER

SCHOLASTIC INC.

New York Toronto London Auckland Sydney
Mexico City New Delhi Hong Kong

CLYDE WAS WORRIED.
Show and Tell was two days
away, and he had nothing to bring
to school. His best friend Rosemary
had brought her coronation Queen
Benjamina doll, and Lawrence had
brought a picture of his aunt, who was
an astronaut. But Clyde had nothing
that special. He rummaged around his
room, searching.

There was a little creature that Clyde
had made out of acorns, with twigs for
arms and legs. There was a gray rock that
looked almost like a heart. And in his
desk drawer there was a scrapbook
of his favorite leaves. Then Clyde
rolled his string collection out
from under his bed.

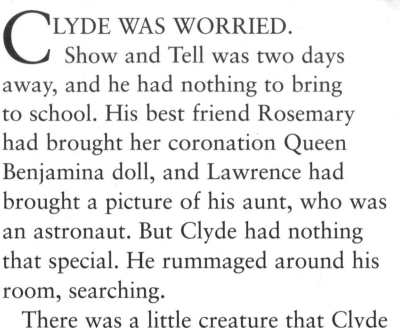

"You're not going to take *that* to Show and Tell?" his older brother Jefferson said with a sigh.

"I might," Clyde said in a small voice. "It's almost the size of a basketball."

"My friend Harry's *is* the size of a basketball."

"Oh," said Clyde.

"Why don't you bring your monster card collection, Clyde?" his mother suggested.

"Every first grader brings monster cards, Mom," Jefferson said.

It was true, Clyde thought.

"What about your leaf scrapbook?" said Clyde's mother.

"Leaves!" muttered Jefferson. "Look, Clyde has to start collecting something special."

"If you love something," Clyde's mother said, "then it's special, and Clyde can tell them why."

Clyde wasn't so sure he could.

Maybe he'd get sick before Show and Tell. He had a queasy feeling in his stomach. "Mom," he called, "bring the thermometer. I think I'm coming down with something."

"You know, Clyde," his mother said, "your great-grandfather used to have a wonderful thermometer collection."

"Where is it now?" Clyde asked.

"Oh, who knows? Probably lost or given away," said his mother.

"What's my temperature?"

"Normal, dear."

Clyde groaned.

At school the next day things got worse. "What are you bringing for Show and Tell tomorrow?" Betty asked.

"Don't know yet," Clyde answered. "What are you bringing?"

"My grandfather's false teeth."

"Cool!" said all the kids.

False teeth! Clyde thought. *That was special all right.*

"What's Ralph bringing?" asked another first grader.

Clyde squeezed his eyes shut and hoped Ralph would bring something incredibly boring. *Please let Ralph bring monster cards,* he whispered to himself.

"A fossil," Ralph answered. "Actually, a dinosaur toe bone. My uncle's a paleontologist. I even have a picture of him digging for dinosaurs."

Clyde nearly cried out in despair.

"Don't worry, Clyde," whispered Rosemary. "I'll help you find something good for Show and Tell."

At recess Clyde and Rosemary
went all over the playground . . .

looking for interesting things
Clyde could bring.

They were still looking when they walked home
from school. But they found nothing. Absolutely zero.
Clyde was getting desperate.

When he got home he decided to look
in the basement for his great-grandfather's
thermometer collection. Maybe it hadn't
been given away after all.

The basement was dark and dusty and
creepy, with cobwebs and shadows. Clyde
hated it. He never went down there alone.
But he didn't want to ask Jefferson to come.

He poked through boxes and piles of old
clothes. Then he saw a round, gray, furry
object. Something just drew Clyde to this
lopsided little ball. When he touched it,
it felt soft and very fragile.

Clyde found a box and placed
the little ball gently inside.

"So, Clyde, the big day is here," said Jefferson the next morning. "What's it going to be for Show and Tell?"

"I'm not telling," Clyde said quietly.

"Oh, that'll be good—not telling at Show and Tell."

"I'm not telling *you*, Jefferson."

"Jefferson, you keep quiet. Maybe he wants it to be private," said his father.

"Or a surprise," said his mother.

"Yeah, a private surprise. That's it," said Clyde.

Clyde walked to school carrying
his box very carefully.

All morning he waited for Show and Tell.
Mrs. McFuzz called on Betty first. Her
grandfather's false teeth were a
big hit. She made them go
chop-chop and let all the
students hold them.

Everyone loved Ralph's dinosaur toe.
It was almost as big as a leg.

Finally, it was Clyde's turn. He stood up and took
a deep breath. "I found this in our basement," he said,
opening the box. "I don't know what it is." He swallowed
and couldn't think of anything else to say.

"It's a mystery object!" Mrs. McFuzz said. "Sometimes
they're the most exciting."

Clyde smiled a little and said to the class,
"It's very fragile, but if you want to touch it, you
can—very carefully."

A hush fell upon the room as each first grader
came up to touch the lopsided furry ball.

When Show and Tell was over, Mrs.
McFuzz put the box on the window sill.
"Well, I think they liked it—maybe,"
Clyde whispered to Rosemary.

But by lunch everyone had forgotten about the
furry lopsided ball. They were talking about Betty's
grandfather's false teeth and Ralph's dinosaur toe.
No one asked Clyde about his mysterious object.

After lunch Rosemary said, "Don't feel bad, Clyde. I think your Show and Tell was great. Let's go and look at your furry ball again." She walked over to the window in the classroom.

"Mrs. McFuzz! Come quick! Clyde, get over here!" Rosemary yelled.

"My word!" exclaimed Mrs. McFuzz.

In the box were hundreds of tiny baby spiders.

"Wow!" Clyde gasped.

"Spiderlings," whispered Mrs. McFuzz. "Come quick, everyone! Come and see Clyde's mystery object."

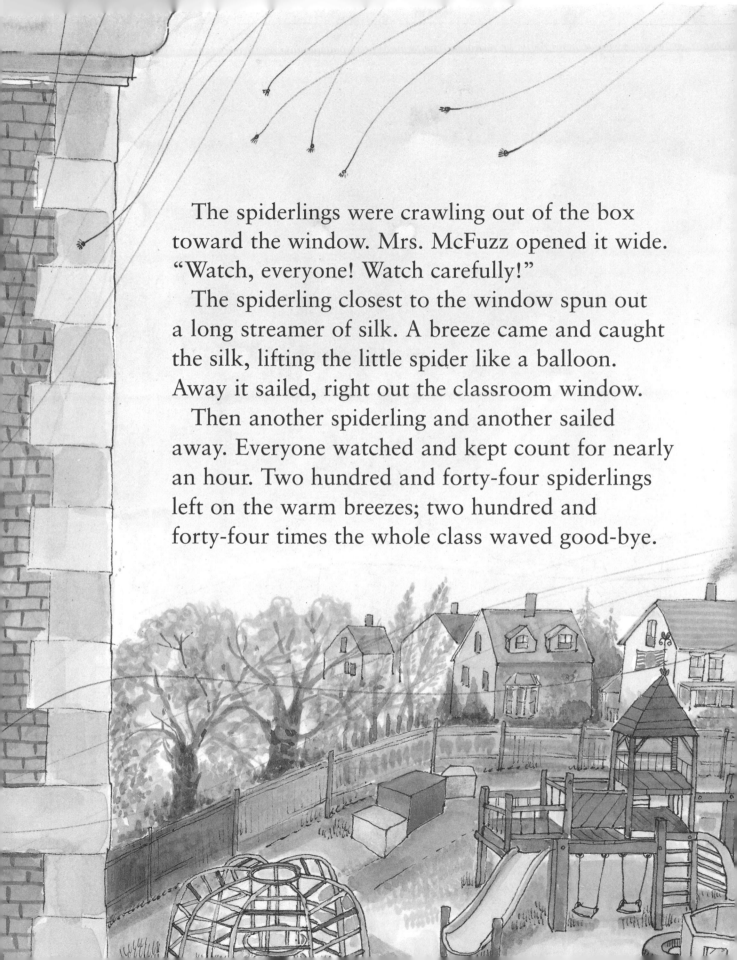

The spiderlings were crawling out of the box toward the window. Mrs. McFuzz opened it wide. "Watch, everyone! Watch carefully!"

The spiderling closest to the window spun out a long streamer of silk. A breeze came and caught the silk, lifting the little spider like a balloon. Away it sailed, right out the classroom window.

Then another spiderling and another sailed away. Everyone watched and kept count for nearly an hour. Two hundred and forty-four spiderlings left on the warm breezes; two hundred and forty-four times the whole class waved good-bye.

No one said another word about Betty's grandfather's false teeth or Ralph's dinosaur toe. All they talked about were spiderlings and spinnerets, and silk and egg sacs. Mrs. McFuzz wrote the new words on the blackboard, and everyone drew pictures of ballooning spiders and copied down the wonderful new words.

"Clyde," Rosemary said softly. "You brought the best Show and Tell of all. It was *much* better than my Queen Benjamina doll."

And Mrs. McFuzz gave Clyde a hug when he said good-bye and whispered a special thanks in his ear.

That night at dinner Jefferson said, "Well, Clyde, how did Show and Tell go? Did anybody bring monster cards?"

"Nope. Ralph brought a fossil—a dinosaur toe bone."

"Wow!" exclaimed Jefferson. "How did they like your private surprise after seeing a million-year-old dinosaur toe?"

"They liked it. It was a surprise all right," Clyde said.

"Big deal!" muttered Jefferson.

Clyde ignored him. He told his family about the furry lopsided ball he had found in the basement and showed them the picture he had drawn of the ballooning spiders. "There were two hundred and forty-four spiderlings in all," Clyde said.

"Goodness," Clyde's parents said together, and they looked in wonder at Clyde. "What did your teacher say about that?"

"Life," said Clyde.
"Mrs. McFuzz said I brought life."

To Liz B.,
a good bunny.—
K. L.

For Lucy, Molly, and Rebecca
and for Sophie and Julia.—
M. H.

ISBN 0-590-51647-7

Text copyright © 1998 by Kathryn Lasky.
Illustrations copyright © 1998 by Marylin Hafner.
All rights reserved.
Published by Scholastic Inc., 555 Broadway, New York, NY 10012,
by arrangement with Candlewick Press.
SCHOLASTIC and associated logos are trademarks and/or registered
trademarks of Scholastic Inc.

12 11 10 9 8 7 6 5 4 3   0 1 2 3 4/0

Printed in the U.S.A.   24

First Scholastic printing, February 1999

This book was typeset in Sabon.
The pictures were done in watercolor and ink.